Care Bears

What Makes You Happy?

by J. E. Bright

SCHOLASTIC INC.

New York   Toronto   London   Auckland   Sydney

Mexico City   New Delhi   Hong Kong   Buenos Aires

ISBN 0-439-45543-X

CARE BEARS is a trademark of
© 2002 Those Characters From Cleveland, Inc.
Used under license by Scholastic Inc.
All rights reserved.

Published by Scholastic Inc.
SCHOLASTIC and associated logos are trademarks and/or registered trademarks of Scholastic Inc.

12   4 5 6 7/0

Printed in the U.S.A.
First Scholastic printing, August 2002

Close your eyes
and think of
something
that makes
you happy.

Do you love playing outside on a beautiful day? That's something that makes Funshine Bear very happy!

Do you love relaxing
and daydreaming,
like Wish Bear?

Does it make you happy to help a friend with a project? Grumpy Bear enjoys helping Share Bear by holding her ladder.

Do you love flying a kite on a perfect summer afternoon? Nothing makes Love-a-lot Bear happier!

Cheer Bear loves to juggle stars and make her friends smile. Do you love to cheer up your friends, too?

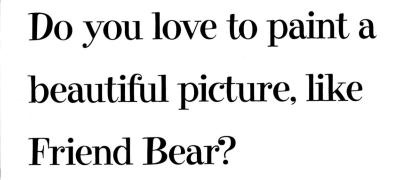

Do you love to paint a beautiful picture, like Friend Bear?

Tenderheart Bear's favorite thing is spreading love all over Care-a-lot. Does telling people you love them make you happy, too?

Is it playing with your friends that makes you happiest? Share Bear loves to rollerskate with Cheer Bear and Grumpy Bear.

Does it make you happy to hope for something good to happen? Good Luck Bear likes to do that— and sometimes what he hopes for comes true!

RAINBOW Trail

Bedtime Bear is happiest when he's snug in bed and having a sweet dream.
Do you love that, too?

Happiness is best when it is shared, so tell somebody special what makes you happy. You'll be glad you did!